Piper Nelid

New York

Sal is at the fire station.

There is an open house.

Sal's family tours the station.
They see where the firefighters
sleep.

They see the radio
where calls come in.

They see the trucks up close.
They have long hoses.

The ladders can become tall.
They can reach high windows.

A firefighter shows them
her special suit.
It keeps her safe from fire.

She shows them her mask.
It keeps smoke out of her lungs.

She lets Sal try on her gloves.
They are really big!

Suddenly an alarm rings.
There is a fire somewhere!

The firefighters get dressed.

They get into the truck.

They turn on the sirens.

Sal waves to the firefighters.
He knows they have
an important job.